TUMBLEWEEDS & COMPANY

by
TOM K. RYAN

FAWCETT GOLD MEDAL • NEW YORK

TUMBLEWEEDS & COMPANY

Published by Fawcett Gold Medal Books, a unit of CBS
Publications, the Consumer Publishing Division of CBS Inc.,
by special arrangement with United Feature Syndicate, Inc.

ISBN: 0-449-14198-5

Printed in the United States of America

10 9 8 7 6 5 4 3 2 1

WHY THE SAD DEMEANOR, WIMBLE?

NOW, WHEN YOU MEET GROVER, MY EDITOR, KEEP IN MIND HE WAS ONCE BEANED WITH A COMPOSING STICK BY AN IRATE PRESSMAN, WHICH SORTA SCATTERED HIS TYPE, SO TO SPEAK.

BOSS, MEET **MOLE-EYE**, THE FAMED SCOUT! WANNA DO A STORY ON HIM?

NO, THANKS... BEEN USING PAPER ALL MY LIFE... TOO OLD TO CHANGE NOW.

WELL! 'TIS THE CAPTAIN, BEARING A MESSAGE! UH, HOW ARE THINGS IN THE GHETTO, OLD FIG?

WE CALL IT THE FORT, FELLA!

OOPS

AND HOW ARE THINGS IN THE WILDERNESS?

WE CALL IT SUBURBIA, FELLA.

I'M BACK, ACE! WHAT'S NEW?

WELL, FOR ONE THING, NOTHING.

OTHER THAN THAT, NOT MUCH.

HUSBAND HUNTER'S HANDBOOK

Feeling neglected, Future Bride? Creating a crisis may force Him to worry about you.

HI, COWBOY. AUNT HILDEGARD SAYS TO TELL YOU SHE'S **VERY ILL**, AND IF YOUR YEARS OF FRIENDSHIP MEAN ANYTHING AT ALL, YOU'LL RUSH TO HER SIDE!

WHAT'S SHE GOT?

AMNESIA

HILDEGARD HAMHOCKER, YOU'RE JUST TRYIN' TO GET MY SYMPATHY! YOU DON'T REALLY HAVE AMNESIA!!

I HAVE SO!

I'VE LOST MY MEMORY, HAVEN'T I?!

YOU'RE FAKING IT!

YOU COULD SEE THE AMNESIA GERMS ON ME IF THEY WEREN'T SO SMALL!

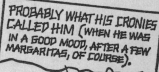

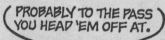

PROBABLY TO THE PASS YOU HEAD 'EM OFF AT.

WHY AREN'T YOU HAWKING YOUR PAPERS, PERCY?

SIGH

AS YOU KNOW, AN IRATE PRESSMAN ONCE BEANED GROVER, MY EDITOR, WITH A COMPOSING STICK, THEREBY SORTA SCATTERING HIS TYPE. SINCE THEN IT'S BEEN DWINDLE CITY.

FOR INSTANCE?

TODAY'S GRABBER:

GET YOUR DESERT DENOUNCER RIGHT HERE! REDUCE EYE-STRAIN WITH LESS TO READ!!

HUSBAND HUNTERS' HANDBOOK

Ah, JUNE! Month of Weddings! In June, Future Bride, you must be like a timid fawn come out of hiding to fondly beckon to her chosen antlered Prince!

TRIVIA MARKER.
This marker was erected
by the Poohawks in tribute
to those Palefaces who'll
stop to read it, and while
doing so, be ambushed.

CHEAP
SHOT!
CHEAP
SHOT!

LO! ENTER, ON THINGBACK, THAT PICAYUNE POOHAWK PEANUT: **LOTSA LUCK!**

HOW'S THE SCENE IN TEENSYDOM, PEEWEE?

SCRIBBLE
SCRIBBLE
SCRIBBLE

RIP!

HOW DARE YOU, SIR. I'M NOT ALL THAT DIMINUTIVE—AND IF I HAD A STEPLADDER, I'D SLAP YOUR FACE.

EXERCISING YOUR HORSE?

YEAH

IT WOULD SEEM THERE'S REASON TO BELIEVE THE TRIPLE CROWN MAY ELUDE YOU AGAIN THIS YEAR.

AH, SHUT UP!

PANT PANT PANT PANT

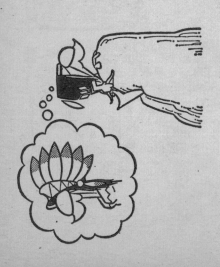

WHEN YOU SEE THE CHIEF, DON'T SAY ANYTHING ABOUT HIS FEATHERS WILTING. HE'S VERY SENSITIVE ABOUT IT.

WELL!? WHAT ARE YOU GAWKING AT? HAVEN'T YOU EVER SEEN A HEAP BIG FUNKY CHIEF BEFORE!?

ADIOS. I'M OFF. <u>THE SOCIETY OF FREE-LANCE GIBBET JOCKEYS</u> HAS CALLED A SPECIAL SESSION TO MEDIATE A POWER STRUGGLE RAGING WITHIN THE SOCIETY.

POWER STRUGGLE?

BETWEEN TREE LIMB BUFFS AND GALLOWS BUFFS. THEY'RE REALLY AT EACH OTHER'S THROATS!

GRIMY GULCH
POP. 49

THAT'S A SWITCH

GRIMY GULCH
POP. 49

"BLESS ME, IF IT ISN'T THE LOVEBIRDS!—HOW FORTUNATE I JUST HAPPEN TO HAVE MY MARRYING MANUAL WITH ME!"

WHAT A AMAZING COINCIDENCE!

WE ARE GATHERED HERE TO...

IT'S A PLOT!

JOIN TOGETHER (AT A SLIGHTLY HIGHER FEE THAN ORIGINALLY QUOTED, DUE TO EXERTION, MILEAGE, ETC.) THIS MAN AND

GEE...WHAT A MOVING CEREMONY!

HAVE MORE FUN
WITH TUMBLEWEEDS

HANG IN THERE, TUMBLEWEEDS	13915-8	$1.25
LET 'ER RIP, TUMBLEWEEDS	13894-1	$1.25
RIDE ON, TUMBLEWEEDS	14040-7	$1.25
TUMBLEWEEDS ROUNDUP	13814-3	$1.25
TUMBLEWEEDS	13756-2	$1.25
TUMBLEWEEDS #3	13672-8	$1.25
TUMBLEWEEDS #4	13683-3	$1.25
TUMBLEWEEDS #5	13789-9	$1.25

Wherever Paperbacks Are Sold